The Time the Play Went Wrong

By Kaye Umansky

illustrated by Kelly Waldek

Contents

PEARSON
Longman

Text © Kaye Umansky 2004
Series editors: Martin Coles and Christine Hall

PEARSON EDUCATION LIMITED
Edinburgh Gate
Harlow
Essex CM20 2JE
England

www.longman.co.uk

First published 2004
ISBN 0582 79640 7

Illustrated by Kelly Waldek (The Organisation)

Printed in Great Britain by Scotprint, Haddington

The publishers' policy is to use paper manufactured from sustainable forests.

1 An Interesting Announcement

It was Wednesday morning and we were sitting in assembly. It had been a particularly long one. Miss Constantinou's reception class had performed some weird thing about nursery rhymes. There had been a long delay at the start, when Mrs Gates couldn't find the piano key. Then Humpty Dumpty accidentally fell off the wall before he should have done and one of the king's horses trod on his finger and he had to be led off, weeping.

Little Jack Horner successfully pulled the plum out of his cardboard pie, but went all stubborn and refused to deliver his punch line – "What a good boy am I". That's all he had to say. Honestly. It's hardly Shakespeare. Everyone was hissing it to him –

Miss Constantinou, Mrs Gates, everyone – but he just stuck his lower lip out and remained mute. He wasn't very good that day, that's for sure.

Little Miss Muffet's spider was made of pipe cleaners and stuck on the end of a piece of string, which got tangled in a music stand and broke, so there was nothing to frighten her away. She cried anyway.

We were all very glad when they ended the show with a rousing chorus of 'I Had A Little Nut Tree' and shuffled back into their places, looking pleased with themselves, although for the life of me I can't think why.

"Thank you very much, children," said Mrs Beard, our head teacher, rising and stepping carefully over the puddles where a couple of the more excitable ones had wet themselves. "Let's give Reception a big clap, shall we?"

Dutifully, we clapped.

"Now," continued Mrs Beard. "We're running over time, so I'll be quick. There's only one announcement: this year's play."

There was an excited stirring. The play is always a popular event in our school. Mr Heggy always produces it and he's really good at drama. Last year we did an action-packed Robin Hood and got our picture in the local paper. I was Friar Tuck, with a cushion stuffed up my front. David Fairweather got the plum part of Robin. I was a bit jealous about that until I found out he'd have to kiss Felicity Downs, who was Maid Marion. But all that's history.

"Sadly, we don't have Mr Heggy with us any more," continued Mrs Beard. Everyone sighed. It was true. He'd gone off to join an educational puppet group, and drama in the school

had been in decline ever since.

"But," went on our leader, "Miss Vine has kindly offered to step into the breach."

Everyone turned to look at Miss Vine, who blushed and kicked over her coffee mug. She was new and wore wafty purple clothes, so obviously we'd christened her 'The Grape'. She had huge earrings and lots of frizzy hair. She taught Class 4.

"This year, we'll be doing Noah's Ark," explained Mrs Beard. "Miss Vine did it in her last school and apparently it was a huge success."

Noah's Ark, eh? Not quite as thrilling as Robin Hood, but I suppose all those animals would provide parts for the infants, if they could just stop weeping and wetting themselves for two minutes.

"Anyone interested in auditioning for a speaking part should come to the hall after lunch," said Mrs Beard. "Speaking parts only, please. Singers and Dancers and backstage people and so on will be called later in the week. That's all. Wait for your teachers to tell you to leave."

Mrs Gates began playing something tinkly, and slowly the hall began to empty. We're not supposed to talk until we get back to class, but we did anyway.

"Are you going to try?" I asked Chrissy, who was sitting next to me.

"Of course," said Chrissy. She'd played Marion's Nurse in Robin Hood. We'd had a comic scene together, and I must say we made a good job of it. We got almost as big a clap as Robin and Marion. (But sadly, not quite.) "What about you?"

"Just try and stop me," I said. "Acting's in my blood."

Well, it is. Gran used to do comic monologues with a concert party back in the dark ages, as she never stops telling us. Besides, my Friar Tuck had been a triumph, even when the cushion fell out. *Especially* when the cushion fell out.

We spent the morning doing maths and swimming (not at the same time). I couldn't concentrate on either. I was too worked up about the play. So was Chrissy. We both had our eyes on the main parts. As far as we knew, Noah and Mrs Noah had enough on their plate without kissing, so there was nothing standing in our way.

2 The Audition

"Right," said The Grape. She was perched on the edge of the stage, holding a sheaf of papers. There was a tape recorder next to her. "Now, I'm sure you all know the story of Noah's Ark. Does anybody need reminding?"

Nobody did.

There were loads of would-be thespians in the hall. Thespians. It's got a nice ring to it. It's a posh word for actor. (I looked it up.) There were the keen regulars, who always audition for anything going; the curious, who were just nosy; some kids who just fancied a change from the playground; and the usual handful of annoying attention-seekers.

I spotted little Mervyn Simpson skulking at the back. Mervyn was a new kid and it showed. He had huge jug ears and a stammer. He usually sat on his own in the playground, nibbling his sandwiches. Rumour had it he was incredibly brainy with a brilliant vocabulary, but it didn't get him far in the popularity stakes. People teased him about his ears, his stammer and his babyish lunch box (Thomas the Tank Engine). Well, he is eight.

"Of course," went on The Grape, "of course, this is a play, so it's slightly different."

"Did you write the script, Miss?" I asked.

"Well – yes, I did, er …?"

"Pete," I supplied.

"Yes, Pete. It went down very well in my last school, but then, we had some very talented actors. Quite brilliant, some of them. In fact, I've never seen such commitment." She gave a little sigh, remembering the sheer genius of the kids in her last school. "Anyway," she continued, briskly, "we'll do the best we can. We've only got four weeks to put it on, so we need to get cracking." She consulted a piece of paper.

"There are nine big speaking parts. Noah, Mrs Noah, their three Sons and their Wives. And God."

God. I'd forgotten about God. Did I want to play God more than Noah? Who had the better lines? Who would be on stage most?

"Noah is much the biggest part, of course," said The Grape.

Right. I'd stick with him.

"Although Mrs Noah also has a lot to say."

Chrissy and I exchanged a meaningful secret glance.

"Then there are seven smaller speaking roles," went on The Grape. "The Dove, the Raven and five Sinners. Some have to dance as well."

"Do the Sinners have to dance?" Dean Duggan wanted to know. He's in our class, and a hardened sinner if ever I saw one. Just ask Miss Archer, our teacher. I was surprised he'd turned up, actually. He's never shown any interest in acting before. He's usually out in the playground, nicking the little kids' crisps or kicking a ball against Gnasher's fence to get the dogs going.

(Gnasher is Mr Nash, our caretaker. He has two dogs called Duke and Hunter who really hate balls banging up against the fence.)

"No," said The Grape. "Just the birds." Dean relaxed. Sinning without dancing. That was just up his street.

"Just remember that you'll need real dedication to take on a speaking role," The Grape warned us. "That means lunch times and the occasional rehearsal after school. There are a lot of lines to learn. Anyone who's not prepared to throw themselves into this can go now."

A few people got up and went at that point. Dean Duggan wasn't amongst them. Neither was Mervyn Simpson.

"Do the Sinners have a lot of lines?" asked Dean Duggan.

"I think I already explained that," said The Grape, patiently. "They do speak, but not that much."

"What do they do, then?"

"Well – they jeer at Noah when he's building the ark."

"What, swear and that?"

"No. There's no swearing. They're just a bit rude."

"What happens to 'em?"

"They get drowned."

"Whaaat? Just for bein' rude?" Dean couldn't get his head around this. He was rude all the time. He was always getting sent to Mrs Beard, but nobody ever suggested drowning him.

"These were biblical times," explained The Grape.

Chrissy's hand went up.

"Yes, er ...?" It must be hard when you're a new teacher and don't know people's names.

"Chrissy. Do the actors have to sing?"

"Well, yes. But they'll have backing from the choir."

"Do the Sinners ..." began Dean, but The Grape cut him off.

"Can we just get on, please? Now, what I suggest is this. I'm going to put on some music and I want you all to be ocean waves."

Blank faces. Silence. Then Roland Sykes, speaking for all of us, said, "Uh?"

"I want you all to think 'sea'. Strength. Storm. Moods. Fish. Rocks."

"He's weedy. He can be a bit of seaweed," said Dean, pointing at little Mervyn, and guffawing at his own joke. Mervyn blushed scarlet. A few people sniggered. Not me, I hasten to add. Well, it wasn't that funny.

The Grape ignored him, which is actually the best way with Dean. She went on talking.

"It's a warm-up exercise. I want you to express yourselves. I did this in my last school and I learned a great deal just by watching how people throw themselves into a role. When we've done that, we'll have a stab at reading. Ready?"

She pressed a button on the tape recorder.
Crashing music filled the hall. Everyone looked at
each other, hesitating.

"Off you go!" cried The Grape, leaping about
theatrically. "Come on! Lose your inhibitions!
Ripple! Eddy! Surge! You're a mighty ocean!"

Sheepishly, we all got to our feet. This wasn't
Mr Heggy's way of doing things. A few of the
girls vaguely swished their arms around. A
giggling posse of Class 3 boys began trotting
around in circles. Little Mervyn Simpson swung
his lunch box. Dean Duggan climbed the wall bars
and leaped off, screaming "Tsunami!" at the top
of his voice, landing on Felicity, who screamed
and smacked him. (A tsunami is a giant Japanese
wave, by the way. Miss Archer was telling us
about it. Even Dean had been interested.)

Chrissy and I looked at each other, shrugged,

and began flailing our arms about, feeling a bit daft.

After a chaotic minute or so of this, The Grape decided to call a halt. She switched off the recorder and we all gratefully sat down again, apart from Dean, who carried on running around humming the soundtrack from 'Jaws'.

"All right, Dean, that's quite enough," said The Grape. You'll notice she knew *his* name all right. Everybody did.

"I'm a shark," said Dean, grinning.

He loves an audience.

"Sit down," said The Grape, rather tightly. "That's if you want to be considered for this play."

Amazingly, he sat down.

"Right. I'm going to hand out copies of Scene One. Everyone get into pairs. A boy and a girl, if possible, although it doesn't really matter at this stage. We'll take turns reading the first bit of dialogue between Noah and Mrs Noah."

I wriggled up next to Chrissy. Everyone else got themselves a partner. Dean made a beeline for Felicity, but she stalked off, tossing her hair, and sat next to David (Robin, remember?). None of the other girls wanted Dean either, so, much to his disgust, he was teamed up with poor old friendless Mervyn Simpson. It was clear from the start which of them would be lumbered with being Mrs Noah. I could see Dean hissing threats into the poor little kid's jug ear.

The next ten minutes were insufferable. Hearing the same lines of dialogue read out by a dozen couples with varying degrees of success is not something I would recommend. The lines were:

Noah:	Ah. There you are, wife. I am just off for a stroll up the mountain.
Mrs Noah:	Well, don't forget to take your staff, Noah.
Noah:	I won't. Where are our sons, Ham, Shem and Japheth?
Mrs Noah:	Out digging up vegetables for tea.
Noah:	Good. What fine boys we have, eh?
Mrs Noah:	Indeed we do, Noah. And we are lucky they have found Rebecca, Ruth and Rachel, their lovely wives.
Noah:	Well, goodbye, dear. I will leave you to get on with things.
Mrs Noah:	Goodbye. Don't be long, it looks like rain.

Stirring stuff, eh?

I can't say I was impressed by the readings. Several Noahs couldn't get to grips with the names of their own sons, and at least three Mrs Noahs stumbled over their vegetables. Dean and Mervyn were spectacularly bad. Dean read in a droning monotone, with no attempt at expression or characterisation. His Noah had about as much life as rice pudding.

Mervyn mumbled. His stammer was just awful, although you could see he was trying. He had particular problems with the letter 'R', which was unfortunate considering the daughters' names all began with it. Every time he ran into 'R' trouble, Dean rolled his eyes, sighed loudly and trod on his foot, making things a thousand times worse. The Grape fixed us all with a look, daring anyone to laugh.

As you might expect, Felicity and David went to the other extreme. They were completely over the top, over-dramatising every line and generally showing off like rejects from stage school.

"Overdoing it a bit, don't you think?" I muttered to Chrissy.

"Absolutely," she agreed. "We can do better."

We did, too. When it got to our turn, we were brilliant. No hesitation, every word clear as a bell and really natural sounding. We even added gestures. We mopped our brows to show how hot we were in a Middle Eastern environment.

"Well, thank you, everyone," said The Grape. "I think I've heard enough. I'll post up the cast list on the entrance hall noticeboard by home time.

"Don't forget, if you don't get a speaking part you can always join the choir or be a Storm Dancer."

"Hah!" sneered Dean Duggan. "Not flippin' likely."

The afternoon crawled by. I wrote a not-very-good story about being a Victorian child mill worker. We were learning about the shocking hours they had to work. Miss Archer said I had to do it again for homework. Some things never change.

When the bell went, Chrissy and I raced to the noticeboard and joined the scrum, looking for our names. There they were, right at the top. We'd made it! We turned to each other and did a triumphant high five.

Here is the list, in its entirety:

Noah – Pete Greenaway
Mrs Noah – Chrissy Johnson
God – David Fairweather
Shem – Ashley Onono
Ham – Rakesh Patel
Japheth – William Higgins
Rebecca – Felicity Downs
Ruth – Emma Saul
Rachel – Mary Malone
Raven – Sheena Wallace
Dove – Parveen Singh
Sinners – Ben Salermo
Gemma Hughes
Katy Crooks
Simon Montgomery
Dean Duggan

Felicity pretended to be thrilled. She kept saying, "Rebecca's the part I wanted" in a loud voice, although we all knew she really wanted Mrs Noah. David seemed pretty chuffed about being God, as well he might be. Noah's Sons

(Ashley, Rakesh and William) were all good mates of mine, so that was a result. I didn't know Sheena and Parveen very well, but I knew they had ballet lessons. The Sinners were all okay, apart from Dean. We couldn't believe he'd been chosen, after all that mucking about in the hall.

"Talk about typecasting," said Chrissy.

"I hope The Grape likes a challenge," I agreed.

Just then, Dean appeared. "Am I in it?" he demanded, shoving his way through.

"Yep," I said. "You're a Sinner."

"Yess!" said Dean, shooting his arm in the air and accidentally on purpose clipping Felicity on the ear.

"Ow!" she went. "Just mind what you're doing, will you?"

"Ah, shut yer face," said Dean, wittily. He turned to me. "You know why you're Noah, don't you, Greenaway?" he said. "'Cos you got no-a brain. Get it?"

"Oh, ho, ho," I said. "Am I supposed to laugh or something?"

"I'll tell you what's a laugh," said Dean. "Your acting."

Smirking, he swaggered off into the playground to terrorise the infants.

He passed poor little Mervyn, who pressed himself into the wall, hoping not to be noticed. He hadn't got a part, of course. You could tell he was fed up about it.

"Never mind, Mervyn," said Chrissy, kindly, as we passed him. "You can always join the choir."

Mervyn said nothing. He just wandered away, clutching his soppy lunch box. I felt quite sorry for him.

Chrissy and I went back to my house to celebrate with Jammy Dodgers and lemonade. Gran was thrilled and promised to help us learn our lines.

What a great day.

3 The Sinner

The Grape was right. There were a lot of lines to learn. True to her word, Gran helped me. Every night we would sit on the sofa with the script, going over it and over it until I was word perfect. Sometimes Chrissy came round. My little sister Molly sat in on our rehearsals. She had our cat Pushkin on her lap and made her clap her paws together at the end of every scene.

There were regular rehearsals at school too, of course. Every lunch time us actors would gather in the hall with The Grape, unless the Storm Dancers were practising their routine, or the choir was going through the songs, in which case we'd do it in The Grape's classroom.

To begin with, things didn't go at all well. Being seasoned performers, Chrissy and I were word perfect, and so were Felicity and David. But several of the others were totally lost without their scripts. The Grape had strong words to say about that.

"I cannot believe this," she said. "Here we are, the fourth rehearsal and some of you still don't know your lines."

"I'm trying, Miss, but I've got a bad memory," said Ashley. This is true. He keeps forgetting the 70p he owes me.

"Well, maybe. But there are plenty of others who would like your part."

"I'll help you, Ashley," I said, out of the kindness of my heart.

Well, I say that, but actually it was in my own interests that the play went well. I wanted my picture in the local paper next to a glowing report.

THE GAZETTE

The audience brought the roof down at Inderwick primary school last night. The amazing cast was headed by Noah, triumphantly played by eleven-year-old Pete Greenaway, whose astoundingly mature performance captured the hearts and minds of

And so on. You know the sort of thing.

"Sinners!" rapped The Grape. "Please, please get your lines in the right order."

"I keep forgetting which number I am," wailed Simon.

"You're Sinner Three."

"But you said I was Two yesterday."

"I didn't. Sinner Two is Katy."

"No I'm not," said Katy. "I'm Four."

"All I know is, I'm One," said Dean. He was sitting on the radiator, making a clumsy paper aeroplane.

"Yes," said The Grape, acidly. "And you still don't know your first line, do you?"

"Yes I do."

"What is it, then?"

"'What you playin' at, Noah?'"

"Wrong. It's 'What are you doing?'"

"Same difference."

"No it is not!"

"Is," argued Dean. Adding, in a mutter, "Stupid line anyway."

"I *beg* your pardon?" You could tell The Grape was furious. Her playwright credentials were being challenged. She was bright red and her earrings were jangling."

"Well, it is. It's obvious what he's doin', innit? He's buildin' a bloomin' great ark in his yard. Any fool can see that."

"Are you arguing with me, Dean?" snapped The Grape. "I do hope not. I was in two minds about giving you a part; in fact, Mrs Beard warned me about your attitude problem, but you seemed keen so I thought I'd give you the benefit of the doubt."

Dean gave a cocky shrug and launched his paper aeroplane. It fluttered down, landing at The Grape's feet. She bent down and picked it up.

It was a copy of his lines.

You couldn't really blame the poor old Grape for losing her rag. Dean had been a real nuisance since day one. He kept holding up proceedings, making stupid comments and messing around. He talked when it wasn't his bit. He made stupid faces whenever God made a speech. Whenever Felicity spoke, he minced around, copying her. He yawned ostentatiously whenever Chrissy and I had a scene.

He flicked pencils. He arrived late. He lost his script. When The Grape gave him another one, he lost that as well. She offered to go through his lines with him after school, but he never bothered to turn up. He insisted that the Sinners ought to be drunk, and brought in a beer bottle as a prop, although we're not supposed to bring glass into school. In despair, she printed out his lines on the computer, and now he'd made them into a paper plane.

"Dean Duggan," said The Grape, all vinegar now. "I've had enough. Get out. I don't want you in my play."

Dean gave her a poisonous look, jumped off the radiator and banged out, slamming the door behind him. Sheena was sent to ask Roland Sykes if he'd like to be a Sinner after all. He jumped at the chance, of course.

And that, for the moment, was that.

4 Rehearsals

With Dean out of the way, rehearsals improved. As time went on, the hall was frequently commandeered by the Storm Dancers, choir or infant Animals, so us actors were usually to be found in The Grape's classroom.

It overlooks the playground. Whenever The Grape's back was turned, Dean would come and press his stupid face against the glass and make chimpanzee gestures, which was highly off-putting. Then he kicked balls at the window. When The Grape finally caught him doing it, she had a word with Mrs Beard. It obviously did something, because he kept away after that, although he still scoffed at every opportunity.

I noticed he was getting quite pally with Mervyn Simpson, of all people. I kept seeing them skulking in corners. Usually, Dean had his jaws wrapped around one of Mervyn's sandwiches or his hand deep in a bag of Mervyn's crisps. I hoped Mervyn knew what he was doing. All right, so he was friendless. But – Dean?

Oh well. It was none of my business. I was in a play, remember?

Things were getting more exciting now. The Grape got out the costume baskets and pulled out everything we used for Joseph, which we did the year before last.

Notes were sent home to parents telling them what their child was and asking for donations of towels, striped dressing gowns and biblical-looking blankets.

Mr Plank, who's good at art, started work on the scenery. Mrs Beard announced a competition to see who could design the best programme.

The Grape arranged to hire proper theatrical lighting for the performance. The local paper was contacted. We don't do things by half measures in our school. We have a reputation to keep up. Besides, the mayor was coming! Mrs Beard read out his letter in assembly. It made me feel quite nervous, but in an excited sort of way, if you get my meaning.

Us actors improved every day. Mr Plank designed a great cloud for God to stand on, and David put on this deep, plummy voice which I thought was a bit overdone but The Grape said was very effective. Shem, Ham and Japheth finally got to grips with their lines. Their Wives had a tendency to overact, particularly Felicity, but The Grape kept them in line. The Raven and the Dove only had one line – "Yes, I will go" – but they danced nicely with an old twig, which was the olive branch. The Sinners, blissfully Dean-free, mocked and jeered like billy-o.

As for Chrissy and me – well. We were great. It sounds conceited, but I'm sorry, we were. Even The Grape said so. She said my big speech on the mountain top brought tears to her eyes. Enough said.

It was a bit chaotic when the various factions joined up and we had the stagger through. (That's what you call it when you go through the play from start to finish for the first time.)

We'd caught glimpses of the dancing and had heard the choir being put through their paces, but it was the first time we'd seen the infants do their thing.

They all trooped into the hall and sat open-mouthed as we ran through the first three scenes.

Scene One was me departing for the mountain and a lot of conversation between Mrs Noah and our Sons and their Wives, followed by a song.

Scene Two was me up the mountain, being given my instructions by God.

Scene Three was building the ark. We didn't have an ark yet – Mr Plank was still working on it. So we just mimed, while the choir sang another song. The Sinners did their jeering bit, followed by yet another song.

Scene Four was the Animals' bit. Miss Constantinou, who is the soul of patience, lined them up in twos at the back of the hall. That took some doing.

You'd never think they'd been practising for weeks. The Grape put on some taped Animal entry music and they began hopping, crawling, stomping and waddling up the centre of the hall and onto the stage. Well, some did. A few dozey ones wandered off towards the playground and had to be brought back.

Was I like that when I was young? I do hope not.

It was really crowded on stage when the Animals eventually arrived. Goodness knows how we'd all squeeze on when the ark materialised. The Grape was manhandling them into their positions, getting crosser by the minute. One of the smallest girls – a rabbit, I think – burst into tears. A kangaroo kept saying he wanted to go to the toilet. An elephant fell off the front of the stage and grazed his knee. Miss Constantinou had to take him to the office for a plaster.

We staggered on.

Scene Five was the flood. The Grape put on the crashing music and the Storm Dancers began cavorting about with lengths of blue cloth. There wasn't enough room on stage, so they used the floor at the front. That went on until they were all red-faced and gasping. Looking at their sweating faces, I was glad I was Noah. I'd sooner learn lines any day.

It took forever to get to the end. No one was gladder than I was when the Dove came back with her twig, the mountain top was spotted and everyone wearily croaked the final song. It had taken us two and a half hours to get through it. The hall was raging hot with all those bodies, and some of the infants were asleep.

"How d'you think it went?" asked Chrissy as we crossed the playground at home time.

"Not bad, I suppose," I said. Well, my bit had been all right. Better than all right. Brilliant, actually. Although I was too modest to say so.

"I expect it'll be better when we've got the scenery. Mr Plank said by Friday. I'm looking forward to the dress rehearsal, aren't you?"

"Oi! Greenaway!" Our conversation was interrupted by Dean Duggan. He was lounging by the gate, a lollipop stick protruding from his mouth. Mervyn was with him. He might have a friend now, but if you ask me he still looked pretty miserable.

"Yes?" I said. "What?"

"Goin' out with your girlfriend?" sneered Dean, staring at Chrissy, who gave him a haughty look and said, "Get lost, Dean."

"I s'pose you think you're good," taunted Dean. "I s'pose you think you're great."

We ignored him and walked on. Like I said, it's the best thing to do.

"Look at 'em, Merv!" he shouted after us. "They think they're great. It's a stupid ole play anyway."

"Shall I hit him?" I seethed.

"No. He's just trying to wind us up. Come on."

"Oi, Noah! You're no-a good!"

Mervyn said nothing.

There was an ice cream van parked outside the school. When I glanced back over my shoulder, Mervyn was fishing a handful of coins from his pocket and handing them over to Dean.

I *really* hoped he knew what he was doing.

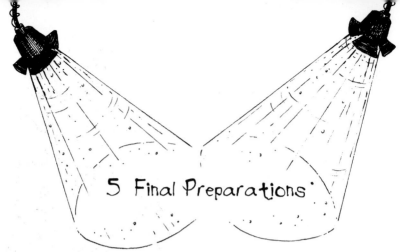

5 Final Preparations

"So how's the play coming on?" asked Dad.

It was Wednesday night. We were all sitting at the table having tea. Mum, Dad, Gran, Molly and baby George in his high chair.

"All right," I said. "It's the dress rehearsal tomorrow morning. The lights are coming. We've got lessons off."

"I must say I'm looking forward to it," said Mum. "When's the performance again?"

"Friday, seven o'clock," I said. "But I've got to be there by six."

My tummy felt a bit wobbly when I said it. Stage fright. All the best actors suffer from it, Gran says.

"You got the bestest part, haven't you, Pete?" said Molly, proudly.

"Mm."

"I'll make sure I'm back from work early, so we

can fit tea in," said Mum.

"I don't know that I'll want any tea," I said.

Gran reached over and patted my knee.

"You'll be fine, Pete," she said. "It's in the blood."

Just then, George upended his plate of beans over his head, so we didn't discuss it any more. I was glad, actually. My nerves were getting the better of me. I went upstairs and played on my PlayStation. There's nothing like zapping aliens for calming me down.

* * * * *

The following day's dress rehearsal was a bit of a mess, but then again, they always are. It was fun seeing each other in costume for the first time, though. Gran had kitted me out in a long brown robe thing and a false beard. I had a staff too, made from an adapted garden hoe. She'd made me put on the costume and practise my lines before the mirror.

The beard took a bit of getting used to. It kept slipping down, so Gran went out and bought some stronger elastic. She was really going to a lot of trouble. I hoped I wouldn't let her down. She kept saying she had every faith in me, which I found quite stressful.

Chrissy wore a striped skirt and blouse thing, with a scarf on her head. So did the Wives and

the girl Sinners. I noticed that Felicity's scarf was flashier than the others. It had little mirrors on. Felicity always likes to go one better. It was a genuine one from the Far East, she said.

The rest of the boys looked like me – bathrobes and so on. There were a few beards, but they were painted on. Only God and I had the full works. Ashley wore his swimming towel on his head. I don't think he's ever washed it.

Luckily, I don't stand too near him on stage.

God was in a white sheet and long silver beard (not quite as long as mine, I noted.) He had a gold-painted cardboard zigzag for lightning. The Raven and Dove wore ballet gear. The Animals had green or brown tights and T-shirts and papier maché masks. One of the deer's antlers fell off, and he cried. Do infants ever do anything but cry?

Mr Plank had done a great job with the set. There was a big backcloth showing sandy desert hills and stuff. There was a freestanding rainbow, which was brought on at the end, and God's cloud, of course. But the ark was a real triumph. It was made in cardboard sections and had to be brought on and assembled before the audience's wondering eyes, while the choir sang a song about rain.

Anyway. The dress rehearsal. It went on – and on – and on. Everything that could go wrong did. David kept complaining he had a sore throat. Chrissy fell over my staff and broke the end off. People forgot their lines, stood in the wrong place, forgot to come on, forgot to go off, dropped props, giggled, tripped over their costumes – you name it. The theatrical lights had arrived, but Mr Plank was having trouble getting them to work. The Grape was frantic.

We'd started first thing after assembly. By playtime, we were only on Scene Two. All the kids who weren't in the play kept coming to sneak looks through the windows. Rather to my

surprise, Dean wasn't among them. All right, so Mrs Beard had told him not to, but that was ages ago. He rarely remembers an instruction for more than five minutes.

I spotted him in a quiet corner of the playground with his new friend. Mervyn was on his knees. He had a felt pen in his hand and was writing something on a big piece of card. Dean was standing over him. He kept glancing around shiftily. I had a feeling he was up to no good.

"What are they doing?" I said, nudging Chrissy.

"What? Who?"

"Dean and Mervyn. Look, they're …"

"Come on, Noah!" screeched The Grape. "Get up that mountain! God's waiting!"

I adjusted my beard, picked up my staff and concentrated on the job in hand.

We reached the end by lunch time. Three hours it had taken us, and it was only supposed to take one. I hoped the audience had a lot of patience. Whatever would The Grape say?

She sat us all down. Everyone was worn out. Some of the Animals looked like they might expire any minute from heat exhaustion.

"Well," said The Grape, "that's it. We're as ready as we ever will be. I'll see you all individually and give you your last notes, but I want to say one thing. You've all worked very hard. They always say a bad dress rehearsal means a good performance, so tomorrow night put all your worries behind you and enjoy yourselves. I'm sure you'll all make me very proud."

That was nice of her. She wasn't a bad sort, really.

6 The Big Night Out

Friday. The Big Night. Oo-er.

It was half past six. The entire cast, plus choir and backstage workers were assembled in the hall. Everyone was in costume. The scenery was set. The lights were working. The piano key had been found. Benches were in place behind the piano, for the choir to stand on. Infant sick had been mopped up. Rows of chairs had been neatly set out by the backstage people, whose names I won't bother you with as they're always backstage.

All the staff who were involved in the play were there, looking a bit smarter than usual. Mrs Gates (music), Mr Plank (lights and scenery), Miss Archer (costumes and raffle tickets), Miss Constantinou (who trained both the Storm Dancers and the Animals and deserves a medal in my opinion), Gnasher (in control of security and infant sick) and Mrs Beard, dressed up to the nines and all of a flutter about the mayor's imminent arrival. And The Grape, of course, who was giving us a final pep talk.

Actually, and you'll be surprised about this, I didn't need it. I'd had all day to work through my nerves, and had finally come out on the other side. I'd woken with a stomach ache, refused breakfast, failed to concentrate in class, given away all my lunch except the chocolate and spent the entire afternoon feeling sick. Then I'd gone home and refused tea.

That's when Gran gave me a big cheese sandwich and a talking to. She went on about doing your best, how you couldn't do any more, how good I was, how proud she would be of me no matter what ... you know the sort of thing. Anyway, it made me feel better, especially when she said she'd got tickets to the circus as a treat for me working so hard. I even ate the sandwich. And some cake.

I felt quite cheerful when I arrived at school with my costume in a carrier bag. Mervyn was hanging around the entrance.

"Hi," I said. "Are you coming to the play?"

"I d-don't kn-know," said Mervyn.

"What about your mum and dad?"

"They c-c-can't. My g-grandad's ill."

"Come on in anyway," I said.

"I m-might."

I felt sorry for him, as usual.

So anyway. There I was, half an hour before
curtain up, all fired up and ready to go. So was
Chrissy. In fact, everyone was. School halls
become magically transformed on play nights.
There's something in the air. At any rate, there
was a very different atmosphere from the dress

rehearsal the day before. Even the infants seemed to know what planet they were on and what was happening, for once. I kept expecting one of them to burst into the inevitable tears, but nobody did.

Our hall has a decent stage, but there's hardly any room at the back of it. The classrooms are miles away, so whenever we do a big performance, everyone involved has to sit cross-legged below the stage, making sure to leave room for the dancers. Not an ideal arrangement, as it spoils the element of surprise. Particularly in Noah, where at one point the infants have to be collected from the front and herded to the back so they can parade down the centre aisle to the front again, in twos. That had gone horribly wrong in dress rehearsal. Still. There was no other way.

The Grape finished her talk, wished us luck, handed out peppermints and told us to take our places. I adjusted my beard, picked up my staff, walked on stage and sat on a stool squinting into the lights. Chrissy went and stood at the side, ready to make her entrance. Mr Plank pulled the curtains together, shutting the two of us off from the rest of the hall.

I took deep breaths, like Gran had told me to do.

"What time is it?" asked Chrissy.

"Haven't got my watch. About twenty to seven, I think."

There was a pause.

"Audience'll be arriving any time now," whispered Chrissy. "Are you nervous?"

"Sort of. Not too bad. You?"

"Terrified," said Chrissy. But she sounded quite cheerful. "Did you hear the fuss in the boys' toilets?" she added.

"What fuss?"

"I was just coming out of the girls'. It sounded like Dean and Mervyn. I think they were having an argument. Dean was saying 'You'd better not do it, Simpson, I'm telling you' and stuff like that. Mervyn was crying, I think."

"Oh," I said. "No, I didn't hear." So Dean and Mervyn's weird relationship was on its way out. I wasn't surprised. I had a feeling it would end in tears.

We fell quiet again, concentrating on getting into role. The Grape's very big on this. You were supposed to sort of think yourself into the part. I thought about being old and living in a hot country with a house full of grown-up children.

Five minutes later, I was still doing it.

"It's a bit quiet out front, isn't it?" said Chrissy.

She was right. By now, we should be hearing shuffling footsteps and scraping chairs and the cheerful chattering noises made by a mighty audience of friends and relations getting their cameras out and rustling their programmes and preparing for the theatrical experience of their lives.

But all was strangely quiet. Mrs Gates wasn't even playing the medley of Noah songs she had prepared.

"Shall I peep through the curtains?" asked Chrissy.

"Go on, then," I said. So she did. Seconds later, she turned and said, "Nobody's here."

"What?" I said.

"Nobody's arrived. Come and see for yourself."

I got up and applied my eye to a chink in the curtains.

She was right. The hall was empty, apart from the teachers and cast. The infants were all fidgeting in their places, clutching their masks and looking bewildered. The clock said five past seven. We should have started by now. But where was the audience?

At the back, the teachers were conferring and looking at their watches, surrounded by a crowd of jostling, anxious-looking children. There was obviously some sort of drama going on.

Chrissy and I stepped through the curtains and up to the edge of the stage.

"What's happening?" called Chrissy.

The infants shrugged. They didn't know.

The teachers continued to mumble and confer. Chrissy and I looked at each other, then hurried down the steps and joined them.

At exactly the same time, Mervyn entered the hall from the direction of the toilets. Chrissy was right. He had been crying. His eyes were all pink. The rest of his face was as white as anything. With his big ears, he looked like a sick rat.

"I don't understand it," Mrs Beard was saying. "The mayor said he'd arrive at six forty-five. The photographer should be here too. Where is everybody? This is most peculiar."

It was, too. Where was my family? They'd promised to come early, to get good seats. So had Chrissy's. By rights, the hall should be heaving with proud parents.

Suddenly, Mervyn, who was hovering on the outskirts, stuck his hand up.

"P-please?" he croaked. "Excuse me, p-please?"

"We couldn't have put the wrong date on the letters, by any chance?" Mrs Beard was saying.

"No," said Miss Archer. "I've got one here, look. Friday the seventh, seven p.m."

"P-please?" tried Mervyn again, but again, nobody heard.

It was then that I noticed Dean. He was hanging about in the background, giving Mervyn murderous looks and making warning throat cutting gestures. He was really beginning to get on my nerves.

"I think Mervyn wants to say something," I said, loudly.

"Not now, dear, we're busy," said Mrs Beard. "Mr Nash, perhaps you'd pop out and look down the road? Maybe there's some sort of traffic hold up ..."

"There's a p-poster on the g-gate," said Mervyn. He spoke quite loudly, for once. He got their attention this time all right.

"What?" said the staff in unison.

"There's a p-poster on the g-gate. I think – I think – someone put it there for a j-j-j-joke or something. It says the p-play's been shifted to the p-public l-l-library.

"What?" shrieked Mrs Beard. There came a united gasp. Gnasher was already hotfooting it out the door, muttering a word school caretakers are not supposed to use under his breath.

"I s-saw it when I came in," finished Mervyn. "It's j-just a j-joke, I expect," he added again.

"The library?" Mrs Beard's face was a picture. "You're trying to tell me everyone's gone to the library?"

"Y-es."

"But it's not even open at this time of night!"

"I kn-know," agreed Mervyn, miserably.

"Someone's put up a poster redirecting everyone to the library?"

"Y-yes. For a j-joke, I expect."

"A joke?" spat Mrs Beard. "This is supposed to be a joke? This is way beyond a joke. Who on earth would do such a wicked, wicked thing?"

Mervyn said nothing. He went even paler and bit his lip.

Just then, Gnasher entered, holding a large piece of card in his hand.

"'Ere we are," he growled, holding it up for everyone to see. "Pinned on the gate, large as life."

On it, in big, bold letters, was written:

IMPORTANT NOTICE

DUE TO UNFORESEEN CIRCUMSTANCES, THE PLAY HAS BEEN RELOCATED TO THE LIBRARY IN ELMFIELD AVENUE.

"I do not believe this!" groaned Mrs Beard.

"Elmfield Avenue's over twenty minutes away. Whatever shall we do?"

That was when Dean piped up. All this time he had been lurking in the background, watching Mervyn take the heat. Suddenly, he saw a way of turning the situation to his own advantage.

"I'll go and get 'em, Miss," he offered. "I know where the library is."

"You do?" said Mrs Beard.

"Yeah. I can be there in ten minutes if I run."

"Well – thank you very much, Dean," said Mrs Beard. She sounded really surprised. Dean being helpful was a rare occurrence. "Shall I write a note for you to take? No, there isn't time. Off you go, then. Explain to everyone that there's been a dreadful mistake and ..."

But Dean was already gone.

"Well, well," muttered Miss Archer cynically to Mr Plank. "Dean Duggan saves the day. Whoever would have thought it?"

"Who indeed?" agreed Mr Plank, who had the misfortune to take him for art.

"Whoever would do such a nasty thing?" Mrs Beard was saying as we dispersed and went to take our places again.

Chrissy and I exchanged glances. We knew.

7 The Play

You'll be happy to hear that, finally, the missing audience arrived – the fittest ones first, followed by the aged and infirm, which included my family. They drifted in in dribs and drabs. Some looked a bit sheepish, some confused and some a bit cross. Most of them looked worn out. Well, they had walked miles and some of the mums were wearing high heels.

By eight o'clock, they were finally settled and we were ready for the kick-off. Mrs Beard made an apologetic speech, promising to root out the culprit or culprits responsible for the mean prank, if indeed they went to our school, which she sincerely hoped they didn't. She thanked everyone for their patience. She thanked the mayor for coming. She thanked Mervyn Simpson for drawing the offending poster to her attention. She also thanked Dean Duggan for his sterling service as messenger. They both got a clap. Dean actually had the cheek to stand up and take a bow. I made a mental note to do something about him.

But not right now. Right now, I had to be Noah.

Mrs Beard finished her speech and gave the signal for the lights to be switched off. The curtains swished apart. The stage lights came up, I took a deep breath – and smoothly launched into my first speech.

"Ah, me. I wonder where everyone is? It's very quiet around here today. You wouldn't think I had a wife and three sons and three daughters-in-law ..."

And so on. I can't write the whole thing out in full, it'd take too long. Suffice to say, it went just fine. Not just my bit, either. Everyone did well. Oh, the odd thing went wrong, of course.

Ashley's head towel came undone, but he played it for laughs, so the audience thought it was supposed to. One of the Storm Dancers got tangled in a blue sheet, but people politely pretended not to notice. A couple of video-wielding parents got trampled when the Animals entered, but that was their fault. At one point, Mrs Gates got her music mixed up and started playing the wrong song, but it didn't matter because they all sound the same anyway.

On the plus side, no one forgot their lines. Everyone came in at the right time. God spoke, the Storm Dancers stormed, the Sinners sinned, the choir warbled and the Animals stayed dry at both ends.

When we finally gathered on stage at the end with the rainbow for the finale, the general feeling was that we'd pulled it off. The audience certainly thought so. They brought the house down, particularly the mayor and my lot. Gran's and Molly's faces were glowing. Mum and Dad were proud too, although I could see they were anxious to make a move. It was an hour later than anyone expected and baby George was beginning to play up.

The mayor made a speech. Flowers were presented to The Grape and all the rest of the staff who had helped with the play, except Mr Plank and Gnasher, who got chocolates.

Then, by popular request, we did an encore of the last song and took yet another bow. There we all stood – the Animals, the Dancers, the Raven and Dove, the miraculously undrowned Sinners, God and me, plus my Wife, Sons and Daughters-in-law, all bowing and beaming while the man from the paper took photographs.

Chrissy and I got the biggest clap. All right, so I'm showing off. The fact remains that we did.

Us kids had to stay behind and change out of our costumes. The smaller kids' parents waited, but us older ones said we'd make our own way home. Dad and Chrissy's mum gave us some money so that we could call in for chips.

Finally, we emerged into the cool night air. Mervyn was just outside.

"You were g-good, P-Pete," he said, as we were about to pass. "So were you, C-Chrissy."

"Thanks," we said. There was an uncomfortable pause.

"It was you, wasn't it, Mervyn?" said Chrissy, sternly. We had compared notes. It all pointed to one conclusion.

"P-pardon?"

"You heard. It was you who did the poster. Dean put it up, but you wrote it. Didn't you?"

He went red. Then white. He opened his mouth, but nothing came out.

"It's okay," I said. "Relax. We know you didn't really want to. We won't tell."

"Th-thanks, P-P-Pete," he spluttered.

As always, I felt sorry for him.

"We're going for chips," I said. "Coming?"

"All right. Thanks. Er – look, I'm s-s-s …"

"Look, forget it, okay?"

" … s-s-sorry."

If ever a kid meant it, he did.

"I said forget it," I repeated, giving him a friendly little punch. "It's hard when you're new. People bully you a bit. But they'll get bored. Just one tip. Get another lunch box."

"All r-r-r-r-right. Th-thanks."

So we took him for chips. He didn't stay long and he didn't say much, apart from 'thanks' and 'sorry' and 'no salt, thanks', and 'sorry' again. Then he drifted off home.

"Poor old Mervyn," said Chrissy, watching him trail out of sight, clunking his daft lunch box against lamp posts.

"Mm," I said.

* * * * *

I expect you want to know about Dean. Did he change his ways, now that he'd redeemed himself in the teachers' eyes and saved the day?

Did he heck. He was just the same as usual. Chrissy and I cornered him in the playground the next day and tried a bit of quiet accusation. I told him that I'd seen him standing over Mervyn making the poster and Chrissy told him what she'd overheard him say in the toilets.

Of course, being Dean, he denied everything. Well, he said, "Ah, shut yer gob, Greenaway, an' go an' kiss yer stupid girlfriend," which amounts to the same thing. Then he went off to take Roland Sykes' last Rolo, which he threw over Gnasher's fence, thus setting the dogs off.

A Sinner to the last.

One good thing, just to end with. The other day, another new kid arrived. His name was Egbert, can you believe! Why do parents do it? Don't they realise they're condemning the poor kid to a lifetime of egginess? He had a Fireman Sam lunch box, of all things. He looked really scared.

At playtime, I saw Mervyn go over to him. They stood talking for a bit. When the bell rang, they went back in together. Eggy looked a lot more cheerful, I noticed. At lunch break, I saw him and Mervyn playing Superman or something with a couple more kids in their class. I noticed that Mervyn now had a carrier bag instead of the lunch box, which was a huge improvement.

Oh. I nearly forgot. The very last thing. The entire cast of Noah's Ark got their picture in the paper, together with a very flattering write-up, which mentioned yours truly by name. Gran cut it out and says she'll have it mounted.

Ashley's head got cut off, but as The Grape said, considering the state of his towel, that was no bad thing.